UNCONVENTIONAL

The Vault

ALEATHA ROMIG

Edited by PRINTED MATTER EDITING

Cover Art by DANA LEAH DESIGNS BY DANA

Formatting by ROMIG WORKS LLC

Romig Works LLC

UNCONVENTIONAL

The Vault

By:
New York Times, Wall Street Journal, and USA
Today bestselling author
Aleatha Romig

COPYRIGHT AND LICENSE INFORMATION

Unconventional

Copyright © 2017 Romig Works, LLC
Published by Romig Works, LLC
2017 Edition
ISBN print: 978-1-947189-13-3
Cover art: Dana Leah – Designs by Dana
Editing: Printed Matter Editing
Formatting: Romig Works, LLC

Author's Note

Over a year ago my friend Georgia Cates and I decided to start an adventure: writing stories that were outside of our brand. Our endeavor was successful on many counts. It opened a world of possibilities and let us shake off the chains of expectation. Though we each wrote different titles, we ventured into that new world under one name.

While that pen name no longer exists, it helped us to expand our horizons and try new things.

The story you're about to read started as a short and sexy, predictable novella written by me as Jade Sinner and entitled HIS TO HAVE, a darker Jade Sinner novella.

If any part of this story seems familiar, it could be because you read the 12K-word short novella. That was just the beginning.

Now, doubled in length, UNCONVENTIONAL is more!

For THE VAULT, I expanded Victor and Erika's story, giving it more angst and emotion with an even more fun and exciting twist.

I hope you enjoy UNCOVENTIONAL!

Disclaimer

This book contains situations involving dubious consent and physical restraint. These situations can be triggers for some readers and erotic for others. If you're willing to refrain from judging these characters until you've finished their story, I promise to make the ending worth your time.

Enjoy at your own risk. You have been warned.

Unconventional
BLURB

Erika Ellis is available to everyone, each night, on their TV—news at five-thirty and again at six o'clock. Viewers think they know her.

They don't, not like I do.

I've watched her—closer than the others—not only on the news, but at all hours of the day and night. I've taken my time and learned her routines and her secrets. I know what she needs.

I'll bring her fantasies to life, even the ones she's yet to realize. I'll be the one to teach her that in submission there is power. She'll understand that she doesn't need accolades from her viewers or the world. She doesn't need to be primped and primed. My praise is what she'll live for. Bound and helpless is where her freedom will be found.

The truth behind the stage makeup and faux laugh is that she is mine—nothing she can do or say will change that.

She doesn't know my unconventional plans.

That's okay.

She will.

It's time to make my move.

I'm Victor Cross, the only man for the job.

From New York Times, Wall Street Journal, and USA Today bestselling author Aleatha Romig comes a fun, lighter story with a classic Aleatha darker twist, Unconventional.

Have you been Aleatha'd?

**There is no cheating in this book. Sit back, enjoy, and please withhold judgment until the very end. You won't be sorry.

To everyone with secret submission fantasies...I promise not to tell

Chapter 1

VICTOR

People try to keep their private information secret, but they don't succeed.

She didn't.

She's in the public eye, available to everyone with the flip of a switch. Turn on the TV and there she is —*Erika fucking Ellis.* Her face, her legs, her entire body there in UHD in everyone's living room, kitchen, or bedroom. Being in the public eye, she should have known better, been more careful. She should have taken precautions.

She didn't.

Her carelessness pisses me off, infuriates me. Yet without it, where would we be?

She let down her guard and spoke without thinking. She isn't the only one who has, but she's the one I've been watching. She's the one who matters.

Obtaining bits and pieces of her life story takes time, but as my mind fills with the possibilities for our future, I know the patience will be worth the reward. The process isn't difficult. It's as simple as standing near her in the coffee shop line.

She concentrates on the menu or the screen of her phone, acting as if I'm not there. But I am, taking it all in.

"Name for the order?" the barista asks.

Close enough to smell her sweet perfume, I hang on her every word.

Suddenly her name is not only announced, but written across her cup.

"Telephone number?" the man at the dry cleaners asks.

A room full of customers and she speaks loud enough for the elderly man to hear.

There it is.

Ten digits that open a wealth of information.

The rest is easy. An Internet search, not even one as comprehensive as done by law enforcement, and much of her information is at my fingertips, just like her hard nipples will soon be.

I dig for more.

Her passwords aren't difficult. The name of her first pet. The dog was mentioned in a personal interview posted by her news station: *Get to Know Erika Ellis.*

That's my plan.

"Ma'am, can you confirm your date of birth?" With a slight change to my voice, I become an account specialist, in need of clarifying her order. "Why, yes, we have this order scheduled for delivery on Tuesday. Will you be available to sign? ...No ...Is there anyone else over the age of eighteen at your residence...?"

Simple questions that in her preoccupied world she answers without thought. Her recklessness is her downfall, and while I appreciate it for the success of my plan, I plan to punish her for it. If I could learn her life secrets, so could anyone, someone, another man. That thought fills me with rage, propelling my blood downward, away from rational thought and straight to my dick. It's painfully hard with the need to take her, mark her, and make her mine. After all, she is. She always has been. I've known it for some time. It's time she accepts it—all of it.

It's difficult to hide my erection as I patiently plan, day after day, week after week, following, listening, and paying attention. Like in the coffee shop, most of the time she doesn't even notice me. Like the song 'Mr. Cellophane,' it's as if she looks right through me, walks right past me. Doesn't even know I'm there.

She's too busy—too preoccupied—to compre-hend that I'm her future, present, and past. Neverthe-less, I'm not deterred. I listen to every word, seize every opportunity. I'm paying attention and learning even when she's unaware. Of course, those times she takes for herself, in her apartment, lost in an erotic novel, she doesn't realize I'm watching. She's too lost in the story. At work, she's too busy meeting every-one's demands. Her priorities are skewed, and it's my job to show her the wrongs of her ways.

Then again, there are other times when she smiles and even says a word or two to me. Times that she's close enough to touch, that our skin brushes over one another's. I live for moments such as those, knowing there will be so many more in our future.

There isn't any question in my mind. With every fiber of my body, I know she wants me too. When our eyes meet or as she brushes past me in a crowded diner, I feel her desire. The connection, no matter how small, is like lightning, radiating off of her like heat from the sun, warming the air and stoking my desire.

In one such encounter, we stand face-to-face, and her pink tongue darts to her lips. Her blue eyes disap-pear as her lids grow heavy with desire. I hear her message loud and clear. I understand what she doesn't allow her words to say. It's her silent accep-tance of what will be—what our future holds. Soon, that pink tongue will dance with mine. Soon, it will beg for my attention as she kneels at my feet.

I know her wants and needs. With those same passwords on every account and every device, I've taken my time to insert myself in her private world. I know the books she reads and the videos she watches on her Tumblr account. No wonder she sometimes seems aloof. She has desires and fantasies that have gone unfulfilled, ones she hasn't shared even with her husband.

Her loneliness is about to end. But like everything in our future, the timing is up to me. I'm the only man for the job.

She's a public figure, and it fucking pisses me off to think that she stars in other men's wet dreams. It's part of the game she plays for the station—perceived availability. It boosts the ratings, but it's fiction. Her availability isn't real. She doesn't belong to them, not to any of them.

She's mine, all mine. I'll be the one who fulfills her desires. I'll be the one to bind and control her. No one else will take my woman to ecstasy. No one else will bring her desires to life—no one but me.

The first day she looked my way and spoke to me —the day our connection forged—I knew we were meant to be together. I've worked my way into her predictable world, and yet she has no idea of my plans, of our future. Her combination of ignorance and arrogance fuels my desire. Erika thinks she has control, she thinks she calls the shots, but just like her appearance of availability on the evening news, her power in our relationship is a delusion, one I've allowed to fester for too long.

I'm a man who needs control. I've allowed her misconception to run its course, but now it's over. My entire body quakes as I imagine the scene: Erika fucking Ellis on her knees, tears falling from her beautiful eyes as she relinquishes her illusion and embraces our new reality.

Staring through the lens at the screen before me, I watch her tits bounce and her perfect white teeth shine. Her lips are full, glossy, and red as they part with laughter.

How am I supposed to keep this camera steady as her giggles ring through the air? Even with my headset covering my ears, the pitch of her laughter can't be missed. The man in makeup with slicked-back hair beside her is a prick. He doesn't deserve her laughter or her words.

It isn't a real laugh that I'm hearing, I reassure myself. It's part of her act, part of her TV personality. It's simply for the cameras, for the audience. Her real rings of laughter, moans of desire, and screams of pain are for my ears only.

My chest fills with pride to know that I'm the only one to hear those, the only one to love her. Let the chorus begin.

Chapter 2
ERIKA

I sigh as I look across the table at my best friend. Jenn's the one who has always been there for me, through thick and thin, through rejection and success. She's my one friend who I feel I can show the true Erika, not the one the cameras see, but the real person under the makeup and hair spray.

The dining room of the restaurant around us is mostly empty. It's nearly three o'clock, late for the lunch crowd and too early for dinner. I'm due at the station in an hour for makeup, but I need this reprieve. I need my best friend, and as always, she's here.

"Babe," Jenn says softly. "A sigh isn't an answer."

"I just don't think I have an answer."

"Do you love him?"

I shrug in a noncommittal way. "I did. When he proposed, I did. When we were married, I did. I think I do. He's like that sweatshirt you've had for so long, the one that keeps you warm and is always there, but it's also different than when you first got it." I tilt my head. "The shine is gone. I mean, after all this time, the spark is supposed to die out, right?"

"No."

"Oh, come on," I say, lifting my brows. "You're telling me that you and Paul still have the hots for one another, the same as when you first started dating?"

"Not the same. Better. We know each other. I know what he likes and vice versa."

"Yeah, I get that, but it's routine. Like tacos on Tuesday."

Jenn laughs. "Really, Erika, when's the last time you ate a taco?"

I look down at my Greek salad, complete with feta cheese, olives, and pine nuts. Even with a few slices of grilled chicken, the calorie count with the red vinegar dressing doesn't exceed four hundred, and I only used a small part of the dressing. After the two-hour workout I had this morning with my trainer, preceded by a two-mile run with my husband, I should be hungrier. However, the mind is a powerful thing. Every ounce on my body looks like ten pounds on the television screen.

Damn high definition is the devil.

"Okay," I admit. "So I don't have tacos on Tuesday, but you know what I mean."

"Mix it up. You could have fish tacos."

I scrunch my nose. "I don't think we're really talking tacos. And truthfully, I don't know if I have the energy."

"To have sex with your handsome, supportive husband?"

"To have the desire to have sex. I'm not sure either of us is willing to try anymore." I sigh again as I use my fork to separate the pine nuts from the lettuce. "It's like there's so much happening, too much to make our relationship a priority." I look up as my pitch rises. "There's a rumor that a local Chicago affiliate is looking for a new anchor. It's the early morning slot, but it's a step closer to a bigger market. It's a giant market compared to Milwaukee. Just imagine a national affiliate. Erika Ellis..." I lift my hands as I say my name. "...bringing you the news from Chicago or New York. The news networks are where it's at. I could have my own show...the Erika Ellis hour on MSNBC or CNN or CBS."

"You know I love you, right?"

"Yes," I answer with a sense of heaviness. This is why I called Jenn. The truth hurts, but sometimes pain is the best medicine.

"You're running away and not facing the real

issue. It's a diversionary tactic that can only work for so long."

"Maybe that's it. The time has expired."

"Erika?"

I drop my fork and look around. No one is close enough to hear us. Nevertheless, I lean forward and speak in a low voice. "The real issue is that I've worked my ass off to be a success in this business. Literally!" I twist my body to look at my own ass, and back to my friend. "I work out. I research. I smile at the damn cameras and show off my stupid legs. Do you know that the damn number crunchers have my skirt length to the millimeter? To the damn millimeter! Too long and we lose ratings. Too short and we lose ratings. Need to keep the men happy and not upset the jealous women."

"I think you're concentrating on your career instead of your marriage."

"We ran together this morning. It's the first time in a week that our schedules have allowed it."

Jenn nods. "Okay. Did you talk?"

"No. I mean we spoke, but we didn't *talk*. It was only two miles, but I had the audible rundown of tonight's headlines to listen to."

"Twice a week, Paul and I go out to dinner."

I humph. "Seriously. It's hard. Someone always recognizes me. It's not like we can be alone."

"Then order in."

"I think I should face the fact: my marriage is

beyond repair. I've failed." I shrug. "He's failed. We both have."

"Since when is Erika Ellis a failure?"

"Do you ever think about things?" I ask, afraid to vocalize my true thoughts. "Things that you shouldn't think about?"

"Are we talking a hot fudge sundae or something else?"

I shrug. "Something else."

"Go on."

"It's that I'm tired. I'm tired of the fight. The fight to keep my anchor seat, of trying to move to bigger markets when there are women five years my junior sitting in those chairs. I'm not getting any younger. I'm also tired of working to save that spark that isn't there. I can only fan the flame for so long. Why should it be up to me?"

"Because you said *I do*. Tell me, has a line been crossed? Has he ever cheated on you?"

"I don't think so."

Her brow furrows. "You don't think so?"

"He seems preoccupied."

"With what?"

"I don't know. I haven't asked."

"Have you ever cheated on him?"

"No. I wouldn't...willingly." I wasn't sure where the last word came from, but it slipped out.

"Excuse me?"

"Okay, I wouldn't. It's just that I have these thoughts, and my husband is damn perfect. He's supportive of my career. He's always there, like that worn-out sweatshirt or a pathetic puppy. Maybe that's the problem. He's too...too accommodating."

"There are people who would kill for a handsome man who's supportive and accommodating."

I fidget with the remains of my salad before lowering my fork to the table and taking a drink of the ice water. Jenn is right. I should be happy with what we have, but I'm not. Maybe it's my concern over my career. Maybe it's that the spark went out and I don't know how to rekindle it. Maybe it's that I've let my fantasies overpower my reality. Maybe it's...I blurt it out, "He wants a baby."

Jenn's eyes open wide. "Shit."

"Yeah." I pick up the fork and go back to moving the lettuce, pine nuts, and clumps of feta cheese around. Though my appetite is gone, in the red vinegar dressing the design is rather appealing.

"Erika, look at me."

I don't. I keep moving the contents of my plate.

Her hand slaps the table. I jump as the silverware rattles. "What?" I look up, knowing my eyes are moist.

"When?"

"He first brought it up over six months ago."

"And now...is that when...?"

I suck in a breath as my shoulders straighten. "With a kid, my chances of advancement in my industry are less than fifty percent of what they would be now. And now, they're not great."

Jenn shakes her head. "Does he know your feelings?"

"Sort of. He said he'd raise it."

"It?"

"The kid."

"That's not an it. It's a person. Besides, I thought the two of you talked about children before you married."

"We did," I say, "but that was nearly five years ago. Back then, we said we'd wait. In his mind, we've waited. I just can't think about that right now. And since he brought it up, every time he suggests...sex...I panic. You know that I can't take the pill and with the possibility of weight gain with some of the other forms of birth control... He's always...I know I'm being paranoid, but what if he made the condom defective on purpose?"

"Do you think he would?"

"I don't know what I think anymore."

"Honey, have you brought this up at the marriage counselor's? You said you're seeing one, right?"

"I haven't brought it up to anyone...until now."

Jenn's head tilts in her understanding way.

I can't believe I'm being this honest. It's cathartic and liberating...and I know what needs to happen. If I can't be who my husband wants and in my heart, he isn't being who I want...who I need, then the answer is clear. I just need to face it. But why does it always fall to me? For once I wish he'd take control.

I take a deep breath and sit straighter. "Thank you for meeting with me. I really needed it."

"And?"

"And I need to get to the station."

"Erika?"

"I know what I need to do. I just wish sometimes that it's not always up to me to take the lead. But it's time to face the facts and move on. I'm not happy. I don't make him happy. We need to come to terms with the reality."

"Maybe if you told him."

"Why, Jenn?" My eyes fill with tears. "Why do I need to tell him? Shouldn't he know?"

"I'm not sure that's fair."

I stand and reach for my large purse on the back of the chair. The restaurant is virtually empty, yet I can't allow Erika Ellis to appear anything less than perfect. I straighten my shoulders and plaster my smile in place. "Life isn't fair."

Jenn stands and gives me a hug. "Call me. You know I'm here for you."

I nod before walking away.

stay current, pronounce every name—even foreign dignitaries'—correctly while smiling in a carefree manner, as if one mistake couldn't get me sent back out to the streets for on-the-scene reporting.

I'm glad there's no pressure.

Keeping the balancing act going with each ball precisely in the air is an exhausting art. I can't help but think about my conversation with Jenn. I'm not ready to face any of it. Though my husband and I aren't lighting up the sheets, there is something comfortable and safe about our marriage. In my earlier analogy, the worn sweatshirt is still comfortable. I need to concentrate on that.

Thankfully, it's Friday and I'm not due back on this set and in front of the cameras until Monday. That doesn't mean I can totally walk away. I have preparation for next week and the never-ending workouts. But for a few days, I can take off the plastic smile and relax.

My husband is always trying to get me to do that. Maybe Jenn is right—that he and I need to talk, but *not* talking is easier. Not facing the demise of our marriage and instead finding comfort in the predictability is easier. Sometimes when life seems too much, we all need easier.

Besides, you'd think he'd understand the pressure it takes to be me, but he never has. Even this morning while we were running, he kept trying to talk. He knew I had the earbuds in my ears. I didn't have time or the energy to listen to him then. We should probably make some time to talk about each other's desires and concerns. What Jenn said is the same as what our marriage counselor has said. However, that one hour once a week is all I can devote to it. If we can't say it there, then it gets pushed away. She encourages us to be honest with one another.

That's difficult when I'm not sure I'm being honest with myself.

I want more.

I want less.

I want to have control in my life.

I want to give it all up.

I don't know what I want. How can I tell my husband? Why doesn't he know?

I never intended to be dishonest with him. What I'm starting to understand, after nearly five years of marriage, is that honesty isn't only about telling the truth, but also about not withholding the truth. I'm confused, and instead of telling him, I'm letting it eat me from the inside.

"Ms. Ellis," Jackie says, "I just got the call—Tamara is ill."

Shit! My weekend reprieve and any time for my husband and me to talk will need to wait. The reality is that I probably would have avoided it anyway. This just gives me an excuse.

My shoulders straighten. I don't want to stay and do the eleven o'clock news. I want to go home —not to talk, but to wash off the makeup and curl up with my Kindle. However, I know that isn't the answer that will advance my career, that will get me out of Milwaukee and into a bigger market. Instead of saying what I want to say, I feign concern. "She is?" And then, I broaden my plastic smile. "I'm sorry to hear that. Does Lonnie need me to stay?"

"Yes. He does. We all do. You'll be helping us all out, Ms. Ellis."

"Not a problem," I say as I notice the cameraman from earlier. His scowl has morphed into something deeper, something closer to anger. I move my gaze away.

Lighten up, Mr. Cross. It isn't like you have to stay, just because I am. The eleven o'clock set has its own crew. Your night is free. I'm the one tied up.

⸺

DEAD on my feet and ready to collapse. That's how I feel as the stage crew untangles me from my wires for the second time today. My feet ache from my shoes though I have only sat while wearing them. Thank God there were no cooking segments at eleven at night. My legs cramp from the way they are perched on the bar beneath my chair, crossed daintily at the ankle.

"Erika," the eleven o'clock co-anchor, Shawn, calls as he is also freed from his microphone and other apparatus. "Thanks for filling in. It's always great to spend time with you. How about I buy you a drink—in gratitude?"

I shake my head. "Thanks, Shawn. I'm beat. I need to get home."

He cocks his head to the side. "Come on, there's a group of us. We always go out Friday night to the little bar down the street. It's tradition. We all need to unwind."

I roll my neck to relieve a few kinks. "Rain check?"

"Well, at least let me or one of the stagehands walk you to your car. The garage is no place for a lady to be alone at this time of night."

"I'm good. I parked close by." I look down at my shoes as I contemplate going back to my dressing room to change. "Of course, I need to do a quick change of these shoes or I won't make it even three feet, much less to the garage. Then I'll be out of here. I hope Tamara is feeling better by Monday."

I really do.

In no time at all, I have my shoes stowed away with various other pairs that stay at the news studio and have my Chuck Taylors laced up. I run my hand over the jeans and top I brought to the station to change into. That was for before, when I thought maybe my husband and I could talk. That didn't happen, and now I don't want to take the time to change clothes. I just want to go home and go to sleep.

As I reach for my purse that's secured in the cabinet near my desk, I see the note:

Don't leave without the red heels.

I swallow as my pulse quickens. Slowly, I turn and look around the room as a chill prickles my skin. No one is supposed to be in my dressing room without me, much less in this cabinet.

Who left the note?

I shake off the uneasy feeling the note gives me, chalk it up to sleepiness, crumple the post-it into a ball, and toss it into the trash bin. Reaching for my purse, I head out.

The hallways clear fast after the late news. There's just a skeleton crew down in the bull pen keeping an eye on the happenings of the world so that the early morning team is up to date. Even the elevator is empty. A short ride down and I'm in the parking garage. I scan the floor where I parked my car. There are considerably fewer cars at nearly midnight than when I arrived in the late afternoon.

I search left and then right.

Where's my car?

Chapter 4

VICTOR

Erika steps from the elevator, still wearing the dress from the set. It's a different one than the one she wore at five-thirty and six. I know because I caught most of the eleven o'clock news live on my phone's app.

She's absolutely gorgeous in the blue V-neck dress and high-tops on her feet as she scans the garage. The hint of panic as she searches for her car adds to my excitement. I want her on edge. I plan to keep her that way, begging for mercy that only I can give.

I narrow my eyes and clench my jaw as the vein in

my neck pulsates. Other than her purse, she's not carrying anything else. Where the hell are the red heels? She had to have seen my note.

Her offenses continue to mount.

I straighten my neck. Erika Ellis has a ways to go and lessons to learn about being obedient. My cock twitches. I'll be her teacher. She's been lost for too long. I won't sit back and watch her unravel any longer. Soon, she'll welcome my tutoring as well as my retributions.

I make a mental list.

First, she agreed to work the eleven o'clock news, upending my plans. I almost lost it right there on the set. Everything that I'd worked diligently to get into place...it was all supposed to start earlier. Instead of making a scene, I told myself it was all right. It would work out. I could adapt. Five hours won't matter, not when we have the rest of our lives together.

When I went into Erika's dressing room, I'd done more than leave her the note. I'd taken her key fob from her purse and moved her car. Since she doesn't need to take it out at all to open or start her car, I bet she hasn't even realized it's missing.

While she was working an extra broadcast, I took the shiny red Lexus back to her apartment and parked it on the street. No one noticed. No one said a word.

The obvious preoccupation that each and every person has with their own life makes executing my plan easier than I imagined. I had considered just abducting Erika from the garage, but if I had, her car would have been left here all weekend. That could have raised questions.

The last thing I want is for any of our coworkers to call and interrupt our plans. This weekend is about us.

As Erika reaches for her phone, I pull up beside her and lower my window. "*Ms. Ellis*, is there a problem?"

Her blue eyes open wide at the sound of my voice. I grimace at the fact that they're still covered with too much makeup. One of the first things I'll do once we're to our destination is scrub her face.

That is, if I can wait to fuck her. Those are number one and two. The order is still up in the air, like my cock would be right now if I didn't have it trapped in these jeans.

"I-I," she stammers, so different from the confident newscaster. "What are you doing here?"

"Making sure you're okay."

Her cheeks pinken as if she doesn't deserve my attention. She couldn't be more wrong.

"You didn't..." She sighs. "I don't know what happened. I could have sworn I parked my car right here." She motions to the row of empty parking spaces. "Have you seen it?"

I hit the unlock button, lean over, and open the passenger door to my truck. "Climb on in. It's too late to be wandering around the garage. You never know who may be out and about."

She looks again at her phone, like she wants to make a call, but then stuffs it back into her purse. "Thank you."

Every nerve in my body sparks at the sound of relief in her voice. I plan on being the only one to give her relief, not only this weekend, but for the rest of our lives.

"You could drive me around the garage." she suggests. "I might have the floor wrong. I don't know. I think I'm tired."

I tilt my head toward her. My time of listening to her direct me is over. Get ready, Erika Ellis: you're in for a ride. "Fasten that seatbelt. We don't want you getting hurt."

She peers at me from the corner of her eye as she does as I say. I inhale her scent. In the small cab, I'm able to smell her uncertainty—her fear—and it fucking turns me on. I don't speak as I maneuver the truck around each curve, down the garage floors to the exit, swipe my badge, and drive us onto the street.

"Y-you didn't look for my car," Erika says as she reaches for the door handle.

I hit the gas. The city streets are virtually empty. I blow through one, two, and then three red lights.

"What are you doing?"

I don't answer, allowing her question and anxiety to hang in the air. My knuckles blanch as I grip the steering wheel tighter. This is what I've been waiting for.

Some traffic lights cooperate while others don't. It

doesn't matter. I don't stop. I don't slow. Erika shifts in the seat beside me but doesn't speak as the tires roll and the miles accumulate on my odometer. The landscape is becoming more remote as the traffic signals grow farther and farther apart.

"Please," Erika finally begs, "I don't know what you're doing, but stop. I want to go home. We're going in the wrong direction."

Just like the streetlights and population, her questions and comments space farther apart as I continue to silently drive out into the country and beyond the city limits. I don't even have music playing. Instead, with only the sound of road noise, I'm striving to hear her thoughts. I want to know what she's thinking, the struggle she's fighting.

As the country night's sky deepens to a velvety black filled with a sparkling of glittering stars, I finally turn to her. Though she's stopped questioning, her body language is screaming. My Erika's body is pressed against the door as far from me as she can get. Her blue eyes are opened wide as she studies me, as if it's the first time she's seen me. We both know that isn't the case.

She hasn't had the nerve to open the door of a moving vehicle, but she's perched and ready. Perhaps the idea of jumping at seventy miles per hour is keeping her still. I hope it's more.

"Where are the red shoes?" I finally ask.

She blinks. The light from my dashboard is our only illumination. "I-I left them at the station."

I turn back to the road as I shake my head and ask, "Did you see my note?"

"I didn't know it was from you."

My palm strikes the steering wheel, causing her to jump and flatten herself closer to the door. "Who the fuck did you think it was from?"

"I-I didn't know. I wasn't thinking about it."

"Just how many men leave you notes in your private dressing room telling you what to wear?"

"I didn't know it was from a man."

I turn her way, smelling not only her fear but also her desire. The sweet scent of her pussy has me ready to take her in this truck and not wait for the cabin.

Erika's head moves from side to side as she makes one more attempt to inch closer to the door. "Please, this isn't like you, Victor. What's going on?"

It's the first time in what seems like ages that I've heard my name from her lips. "So I'm not *Mr. Cross*?" It's what she calls me at the station.

"You are. That's your name."

"And yours is Erika *Ellis*?"

"Victor, I don't—"

I cut her off. "Sir."

Her shoulders straighten. "What?"

"No names this weekend. You may address me as Sir."

"I-I may *what*? I will not—"

We are now out of the city and smack dab in the middle of nowhere. Buildings and even houses are a thing of the past. Soybean and cornfields cover the countryside. Thin rows of trees line the open fields next to grassy ravines that meet the narrow gravel shoulder. The moon is barely a sliver. One wrong move during a dark night's drive and the truck could end up in a five-foot-deep gulch. Thinking only about the woman in my truck, I stomp on the brake and pull the truck to the shoulder. The tires squeal and the undercarriage pings as rocks and gravel fly. Faster than Erika can process, I throw the truck into park, unbuckle my seatbelt, and slide next to her, pinning her between me and the door.

The heat of her body radiates to mine as her breathing deepens.

"Don't even think about opening that door," I warn, my voice more of a growl. "There's a five-foot drop out your door and if you fall, I'll follow your fine ass down and take you right there in the mud."

She swallows, her frightened eyes staying fixed on mine.

With one hand in her hair at the nape of her neck and the other possessively splayed over her upper thigh, I pull her toward me. Between the door and her seatbelt, she's trapped.

"Sir," I repeat. "Your only other option is *Master*."

A tear teeters on her lower lid until she blinks, and it dangles from her overly thick mascara-covered lash. "Vic—"

I pull her lips to mine. Her hands ball into fists as she shoves against my chest. I'm too big, too strong, too determined. With her finally in my arms, I take what belongs to me, abusing her mouth with mine. Without hesitation, my tongue plunges into her warm, sweet haven, searching and probing. Her tiny fists pound as my chest crushes her tits. The thump of her heartbeat drums below mine. Her fear and arousal fill the air, a sweet, intoxicating aroma that instantly turns my cock from hard to steel.

With my fingers winding into her brown hair and unashamedly yanking her head back, I continue to hold her lips captive. Kiss by kiss, her pleas soften. The more I probe, unrelentingly bruising her mouth, the more her muscles relax, and her body melts against mine.

When I finally pull back, our gazes lock, and I silently dare her to speak. When she doesn't, I reach for her hand. Erika tries to hold it back, but I'm not in the mood for negotiation. Taking her hand, I push her palm against the front of my jeans, rubbing it over my throbbing erection. "Feel what you do to me?"

When she doesn't answer, I pull her hair again, wrenching her neck backward, causing a gasp to fall from her lips. "Do you feel that?" I ask again.

"Y-yes," she whimpers.

My lips curl upward. "Yes, what?"

"Yes, *Sir*."

Chapter 5

ERIKA

Oh dear Lord, this can't be happening.

I close my eyes, hoping to block everything out, but I can't. Victor continues to rub my hand over his erection—over his large, hard, angry cock. I've never seen him like this. He's not the cameraman who watches me, the man I've known for a while. He's possessed.

"Say it again," he demands.

"Yes, Sir." My voice isn't my own. It's weaker and submissive.

I've never been submissive in my life.

"Say what you do to me."

My scalp stings as his hold of my hair intensifies.

"I make you hard." When his dark eyes narrow, I add, "Sir."

Victor releases my hand and moves his under the hem of my skirt. Every nerve in my body is on fire. There are flames scorching places within me that I never knew existed. The fatigue from the station is gone, replaced with adrenaline coursing through my bloodstream at record speed. The higher his fingers move, the more I'm electrified.

"Please..." I'm not sure what I'm asking. This isn't right. It's not the way it should be.

His fingers inch up my thighs, causing me to shudder at his forwardness. He's touching me, and I'm exposed, only a thin layer of material between him and my core. Why didn't I change before I left the station? In jeans, he couldn't touch me. In jeans, I'd be safe.

But would I?

I gasp as he brushes the crotch of my panties.

"Kitten, you're soaked."

Kitten?

"You're soaking wet," he repeats. "You want me to put my hard cock in your pussy in that dirty ditch, don't you?"

"No!" I say, appalled by his language—words I've never heard him or any man utter—as I try to close my legs and stop his invasion.

He's too strong. His finger curls under the cotton crotch and teases my clit, sending shock waves crashing through me. Despite my verbal protests, one finger and then two find their way between my folds. I try not to moan, but my body is clenching his fingers, holding on tight.

"P-please," I plead. "Please don't do this."

"You want it. You want it bad."

"No, I don't."

My head jerks back and I screech in pain as he pulls my hair again, this time causing tears to trail down my cheeks.

To my utter shock, Victor sticks out his tongue and licks my face, from my chin to my eye. I try to back away, but I can't. He does it again, his spearmint-scented breath in my nose as his saliva covers my cheek. All the while his fingers continue to assault me, to plunge in and out of me.

"Cry, kitten," he says. "I'll drink every tear, each drop making me harder. Each one is another thrust in your pussy because you're going to relieve this ache in my cock. I'm going to take you in ways you've never imagined." He glances down to where his hand is under my dress. "Look at how you're rocking your hips to my touch. You want this. You want me. You're mine, and you always will be." He sits straighter, looking directly into my eyes as his fingers still. "You know that, don't you?"

I'm not sure what I know, embarrassed that my body is reacting—no, appalled. This is wrong, and yet

I was moving with his fingers, wanting him to touch my clit, needing for more than what he's giving me.

Another long lick of my face, and I fight to not flinch. "Tell me," he demands.

"What? Tell you what?"

My head snaps back again, my scalp screaming from the repeated attack.

"Don't make me punish you," Victor warns.

Punish me?

"Hurting you is my goal only to bring you pleasure, but if forced, I'll do it for punishment too, kitten. I'll make you cry. I'll make you scream. Follow my rules and this will go much better for you."

His rules?

His fingers leave my core. But before I can think about the loss of his touch, cool night air and the truck's AC reach my chest as he rips the front of my dress, pulling it apart at the seams.

"That's the station's..."

My words fade away as he hisses at the sight of my breasts, pushing up out of my lace bra.

"This is what you wear to make the men of Milwaukee hard?"

"No..." I shake my head.

Without removing my bra, Victor pushes the lace cups down, exposing my breasts.

He leans forward and catches one nipple between his teeth. Shock waves ripple to my core as it elongates.

"Look at your nipples," he teases. "They're hard as rocks. You're turned on. Now tell me what I want to hear. Tell me who you belong to."

I don't want to look. I can feel how my nipples are betraying me. Instead, I look him in the eye. "M-my husband." It's not the answer he expected, but it's the truth. For now, I do.

He pinches my other nipple, and I shriek at the jolt of pain. "Try again, and don't forget to say Sir."

""I do, Sir. I belong to him. I'm married."

"Does your husband know that? Have you told him? Does he make you wet?" Victor sucks on the finger that was only moments ago inside me. "Does he make you this wet?"

I can't process all of his questions. My husband can make me wet. He has. I nod.

"Then why did you choose to keep him waiting? If you wanted him, you wouldn't work an extra broadcast, would you?"

"I-I...it wasn't about him."

He tweaks my nipples, pinching them roughly with his fingers. "Oh, kitten, it should be, but since it's not, you've got me. I'm going to teach you how to treat a man."

"Please..." It's all I can think to say.

Victor leans back, giving me space for the first time since the truck stopped. "Take off your underwear."

"What?"

His fingers roughly squeeze my cheeks, crushing my mouth against my teeth until the taste of copper lets me know it's bleeding. "Sir," he says. "Don't make me say it again."

I nod. When he releases my face, I move my jaw from side to side before I say, "Yes, Sir."

He sits back again, never taking his eyes from me while I shimmy out of my panties. It's not an easy process in a torn dress and confined by the seatbelt.

"Give them to me."

My pulse races as I hand him the light pink panties that match the bra still under my breasts.

Victor takes my panties to his nose, closes his eyes, and inhales. He sighs. "I love your scent. But I never knew that you'd be so fucking wet." And then his dark eyes are back on me. "If you forget to say *Sir* one more time, these are going in your mouth. Do you understand?"

I shiver at the thought. "Yes, Sir."

Who the hell is this man?

His cheeks rise as his lips curl into a cruel smile. "That's my pet. Before we're done, you're going to not only know who you belong to, but you'll say it too."

I don't answer as he scoots back to the driver's seat and fastens his seatbelt.

When we're done? That's what he said. Will he let me go? Will I get back to the man I married, the kind man who would never do this to me?

As I reach for the cups of my bra, Victor stops

me. "Don't cover yourself. I want to look at you, at your hard nipples. I want to know that all I need to do is reach out to get your attention." He reaches over and rolls one nipple between his thumb and finger, eliciting a gasp.

I bite my lip to stop the moan that is perched ready in my throat.

"I plan to keep you naked all weekend," he says.

Silence falls over the truck as I try to comprehend what is happening. But I can't. It's more than I can process.

"When we get there," he continues, interrupting my thoughts, "the first thing I'm going to do is fuck that smart mouth of yours. You like telling people what to do, don't you?"

Let him try. I'll bite.

I don't answer him. This is ridiculous. He can't talk to me like this.

Still holding my panties, he lifts his chin and puts the truck into drive. We ease back onto the road. For not the first time, I entertain the idea of escaping, but to where? We're in the middle of nowhere. There isn't a soul around. Not even one car has passed his truck since he pulled over. I bet my phone doesn't even have a signal.

My eyes dart to my purse.

Victor reaches it before I do, pulling my phone from the cavernous inside.

"No, kitten. This weekend is just about us."

Pushing the power button to turn it off, he stashes it in the glove compartment. His dark eyes momentarily turn my way. "Remember, follow my rules or be punished."

I'm dumbfounded.

"You think that because you're on people's TVs," he continues, his voice deep and threatening, "that you're better than everyone else, don't you?"

"No, Sir."

Victor snaps his eyes in my direction and then back to the road. "Don't lie, kitten. I'll punish you for lying—every time. Don't forget that. Consider this your one and only warning. I've seen you. I've watched you. You think you're special." He lifts my panties and inhales again. "You're right."

"I am?"

"You're special to me. Only to me. You're everything to me. You're whatever I want you to be: *my* slut, *my* whore, and the love of my life. We'll be together forever."

I shudder at his words: slut, whore. They aren't right. Forever?

"I'm going to make you mine in every way."

It's wrong that my thighs are growing slicker with his nasty adjectives. My husband would never talk like that. Compliments and endearments—that's what he's always spoken. It's what every normal woman would want, yet Victor's cruel words are twisting my insides in an unfamiliar, painful, yet erotic way, drenching my core.

"I'm going to not only fuck your mouth, but all of you—everywhere."

My eyes grow wide as I hear his meaning. "No. I can't. I've never."

Victor grins. "You will, you are. Say *'yes, Sir.'* Tell me I can fuck your ass."

Chapter 6

VICTOR

I've wanted her ass for as long as I can remember. The way it shimmies in the dresses on the set. The way she shows off her legs and teases everyone with the tight skirts. Sure, she's married, but I'm certain that tight, puckered hole has never had a cock buried deep inside of it.

It will. It will forever. My cock will be deep in her ass.

The cab of the truck grows quiet as I let her think about my promises, as she reflects on our new relationship, and as I let her contemplate how things have changed. My plans may be unconventional, but the conventional hasn't worked. She's ignored me for long enough—treated me like I didn't exist. This is our future.

I steal a glance her way. The thick makeup from the set is stained from her mascara tears. She's mulling over my threats and promises. I can sense it in the way she stares out at the narrow strip of light illuminating the direction we're headed. She has to know that she can't stop us now.

I don't force Erika to answer, to tell me that I can take her everywhere, because when Erika tells me that her ass is mine, I want her to mean it. I want her to beg me to fuck her, hard and raw. She's going to beg for it, and when she does, she'll be mine to have.

"Where are you taking me?" Erika finally asks.

"Oh, kitten, I'm taking you to a remote place where no one will hear you scream."

"Please, Vic—Sir," she quickly corrects. "Please, take me home. We can forget this ever happened. I won't say a word—"

"You're right. You won't say a word unless I let you."

Her head moves from side to side as she turns toward the window. With time, her self-righteous posture bends to the inevitable. From her body language, she's telling me that she's accepted her fate. I just don't know how that translates to her actions.

It takes another thirty minutes, but finally I turn

off the country road onto a lane of gravel under a canopy of trees. The cabin is at least half a mile from the main road—main being a relative term. It's far enough back that with the trees, unless you knew it was there, you'd never find it.

I'd been here the day before, preparing for our arrival.

Ms. Erika Ellis may have delayed our road trip, but she couldn't have escaped her fate if she'd tried.

I pull the truck alongside the rustic old cabin and turn toward Erika. "Welcome to your new home."

She doesn't move as I open my door. When I reach her side of the truck to open her door, she remains perfectly still. "Come now, kitten, I don't think I've ever seen you speechless."

"Please, V—Sir, please don't make me go in there. This will change everything. Take me back to town before this goes too far."

I offer her my hand as if we're about to dance, and in a way, we are. "Yes, kitten, this will change everything. When this is done, you'll know you're mine—forever."

Her hand trembles as she places it in mine. It's small enough that I wrap my fingers totally around it, encasing it, keeping it and her for me. She looks down as the soft summer breeze blows against her exposed tits.

"That's right. Look at your hard nipples. You may be saying you don't want to go in there, but your body is saying you do."

She doesn't respond.

As soon as we're inside, I plan to remove all of her clothes. Not only her tits but her body—her *entire* body—will be at my disposal the whole time. Her steps are small, unsure, a complete contrast to how she usually prances around. I've watched her at the station, moving around the city, and even in her apartment. This uncertainty is new and hotter than I imagined.

I open the front door, lead her inside, and hit the light switch. Thankfully, I'd turned on the generator the day before. The air is cooled, but not too cold, and the large main room floods with light.

Erika stalls, her mouth opening as her feet forget to move. "No. Please." Her words are meant for me, but her eyes are too busy scanning the room. It isn't the small kitchen area or table that has her attention. It's the St. Andrew's cross secured against one wall, a bondage table nearby, and an elaborate hook and chain suspended from a ceiling beam. Below the suspended chain are two large rings set in the concrete floor and connected to ankle cuffs.

Near the cross on one wall is an armoire. She doesn't know what it contains, but I know that it's filled with every toy and accessory imaginable. Next to it, in plain sight hanging on the wall, is an assortment of whips, crops, paddles, floggers, and canes. I know she isn't ready for all of this, and I'd considered putting it away, but I couldn't resist seeing her reaction.

She barely blinks as she takes it all in. And then her body remembers how to move as she turns slowly toward the large four-poster bed already adorned with wrist and ankle cuffs.

Erika swallows as her lip disappears behind her teeth, and the pink leaves her cheeks. Her grip upon my hand tightens.

I pull her close and menacingly whisper near her ear. "I know your fantasies."

She shakes her head.

"What did I say about lying?"

"I've never said..." She can't seem to take her eyes off everything.

"I've seen your Kindle account. I know what you like to read. Your Tumblr account. I know what videos you watch." My smile broadens as I take a step back and release her hand. "You're a dirty slut. Those books and videos make you hot, so hot you've gotten yourself off. You think I don't know. I do. I know that you want to be treated like my property, and that's convenient because that's what you are. You are mine —no one else's. Mine."

Her gaze falls to the floor as she bites her lower lip. "I do read and watch. That doesn't mean that I want to live..."

I have no desire to debate this with her. "Take off your clothes, everything."

I step back to the outside door and latch it. "I'm locking the door to keep us safe inside and to keep us from being interrupted, not because I'm worried about you running. You know how long we drove to get here. Tell me, kitten, do you think you can run away?"

"N-no, Sir," she says, fumbling with her torn dress.

"That's good because if you did and I caught you, I'd punish you until you couldn't sit or stand, and then I'd fuck you in every way possible. Is that what you want?"

The dark river of tears is once again flowing. "N-no. S-sir."

Her words are separated by soft cries. I resist the urge to lick the salty liquid from her cheeks. It isn't that I don't want to taste her fear, but that I honestly worry that if I supply any more stimuli, it might send her over the edge. This is a bold new world, and my kitten is barely keeping up.

Once her clothes and shoes are off, I begin her education. Lesson number one: follow directions. I point to the large circle in the beam and the chain hanging from it. "Remember those shoes you were supposed to bring?"

She only nods.

I look down at her bare feet and shake my head. "Your toes are going to get tired."

Her expression blanks until she comprehends my meaning. She understands that binding her from that chain with only her toes touching the floor would have been easier with the four-inch red heels I told her to bring. "P-please...I didn't know...how could I know...?" Her words trail away as her shoulders drop. Her body is telling me that she realizes there's nothing she can beg for. Everything is at my discretion.

"You don't need to know. You need to trust, obey, and submit." When she doesn't respond, I point to the floor. "Kneel."

Her eyes dart to the St. Andrew's cross as her chest heaves and she falls to her knees.

"Good girl," I praise as I walk closer. "Eyes down, always down." I tilt her head forward. "I want that ridiculous makeup gone, but first, I made you a promise." I unsnap my jeans and sigh. The relief at freeing my hard, throbbing cock is overwhelming. Having Erika Ellis naked on her knees has been my fantasy, and it's now my reality.

When she looks up through her lashes, seeing me stroking my cock, she gasps. "No." Her one word is laced with a familiar smugness in her tone. She lifts her chin. "You can't make me. I'll bite it off. I swear I will. This is ridiculous. I'm not sucking you like this."

"Kitten," I purr, stroking her hair and tilting her eyes back down. "I never said you were. I said I was going to fuck your mouth."

She starts to stand when I push her back to the floor. "Do not move without my permission. Eyes down."

I wait until she sinks again to her knees and bows her head before I walk over to the armoire, the one I thoroughly stocked the day before. While I would like her to willingly submit, I have to admit that her fire is erotic. It always has been. Searching through the toys, I find wrist cuffs and a spider gag, items I thought I might need.

Still fully dressed, minus my unbuttoned jeans and pulled-down boxers, my cock hard and pointed toward the sky, I take my choice of toys back to my kitten. Walking around behind her I say, "Put your hands behind your back."

"Vic—"

I wrench her head back again by her hair.

"Sir...p-please," she rephrases with more tears.

She doesn't say more as I release her hair, bend, and lick away her tears. "Hands behind your back."

Her shoulders sag as she complies. The cuffs are lined with sheep's wool and won't hurt her or her skin, no matter how hard she pulls. The buckles keep the cuffs tight and her wrists together. "Lift your head."

It's then she sees the gag and her blue eyes fill with unbridled fear. It's a more beautiful sight than I ever imagined.

"What's that?"

I pet her hair. "I told you, it's not your place to understand or question. It's your place to trust my word. I said I was going to fuck that smart mouth. That's what I'm going to do. I'm not taking the chance on you biting me."

She shakes her head. "No, please. I don't want that thing. I won't bite. I won't."

"Open your mouth, kitten. I've imagined this between your sweet lips."

When she holds her lips together, I pinch her nose. It only takes a few seconds for her to gasp for air. When she does, I slide the metal gag between her teeth. "Don't fight it. I don't want to hurt you."

Her eyes widen as I attach the gag to an elastic band that secures around her head. The gag has a ratchet-like lever, and click by click, her mouth opens until she moans. "Oh, kitten, that's perfect. Now you're going to let me fuck that pretty mouth. Agree, or I'll open it wider."

Quickly she nods her agreement.

I smile as she tries unsuccessfully to talk. The gag holds her tongue in a way that makes her words only sounds—erotic and frantic sounds—encouraging me to fuck her mouth.

"That's it. Don't worry. I'm going to do it. You don't need to beg." After a few more strokes as my balls tighten in anticipation, I plunge my dick between her pried-open lips. It's not the same as it would be to have her lips closed around me, but the ring creates friction and her mouth radiates warmth. I wrap my hands in her hair and thrust. With each plunge, I push deeper as my tight balls bounce off her chin. In and out, until the sound of her gagging pushes me over the edge.

Instead of coming in her mouth, I pull back. One more stroke. I grasp her hair with my other hand, keeping her in place as stream after stream of my sticky white cum rains over her. She closes her eyes and attempts to turn away as it shoots in her opened mouth, her hair, and down her tits. When I release her hair, my kitten's head falls forward, my cum combining with her drool dripping from her chin.

She's so fucking sexy like this. It's not the Erika the viewers see.

Knowing that I'm seeing a side of her that no one else does keeps my dick hard. I lift her by the arm until she's standing and back her, step by step, toward the bed. She still can't talk, but by the tenseness in her muscles, I can sense that she's fighting to look at me, glare at me, even yell at me, but at the same time, the submissive part of her, the part she's hidden away, wants to be obedient and keep her eyes downcast.

Her internal struggle is like a shot of Viagra to my bloodstream.

Chapter 7

ERIKA

My spit mixes with his cum as it drips from my chin. I can't swallow with this thing in my mouth, not really, not with the way it pushes on my tongue. I want to beg him to remove it, to take it off. I want to scream and tell him he's a monster, and at the same time, I have to admit that I want him to fuck me. As he pulls on my arm, making me stand, all I can think about is his cock, not in my mouth, but inside me. Though this is all kinds of wrong, I've never been so wanton.

My legs collide with the bed as he moves me

backward. He doesn't stop until I fall onto my bound hands, onto my back, and onto the mattress. I make the only sounds I can as I come to a stop.

"Spread your legs."

I can't physically fight him, even if I want to. But my pride won't let me submit. I hold my thighs together, knowing that if I obey, not only am I allowing him to see me, but he'll also see how turned on I am.

Despite this terrible place he brought me and all the things here, all I can focus on is him. My gaze scans him from his long muscular legs up his toned body, his handsome face, all the way to his dark hair. When our eyes meet, I remember what he said, and lower my gaze.

He's tall, at least ten inches taller than me. He probably outweighs me by nearly a hundred pounds, not of fat but of muscle. He's a brick house, and I'm no opponent. His fingers dig into my thighs as he pries them apart and easily lifts each of my feet to the bed. I turn my eyes away in shame as he continues to spread my knees, exposing my core.

"Holy fuck, kitten, you're soaking wet. Your cum is dripping all the way to your asshole. Damn, you're needy."

He brushes his finger around my tight muscled ring and I writhe. I can't talk. All I can do is grunt.

"I know your tight hole wants my cock, but, kitten, you're going to need to wait—wait until you beg for it."

His touch moves upward, his fingers plunging. It's heaven and hell. With my hands behind my back, my ass is lifted. Though, my mind says to fight, my body wants what only Victor can give me. All I can do is arch my back, praying he'll go deeper, praying he'll pleasure my clit.

"That greedy cunt wants my cock, doesn't it?"

I can't believe how he's talking to me. I've never heard him speak this way. I shake my head, unwilling to tell him the truth.

Victor grimaces before he says, "Kitten, I warned you. Don't move."

I shiver at the loss of his touch as he leaves me with the combination of my spit and his essence cooling on my skin. The echoing of his footsteps tells me that he's walking back to where he found this gag. I pray he's not going for the crops—or, God forbid, the canes. I've only read about them, but from what I've read, I don't think I can take a cane.

When Victor returns, he lifts my ass higher and slides something underneath me. It's as if I'm a baby and it's a diaper. It takes me a second to realize that it's a chastity belt. He's locking away my core...my clit.

I groan as the padlock clicks.

"Put your feet back on the ground," he commands. "We're going into the shower and wash that shit from your face."

When I stand, Victor does something to the gag —touching a side lever that releases the pressure and lets my mouth close. The immediate relief causes me to sigh. Once the gag is fully removed, Victor holds my arm and stares down at me. I try to keep my eyes down until he says, "Look at me, kitten."

I do, but my gaze is veiled. In the last few hours the man with me has changed. He's so much taller, and his shoulders are broader than I realized. He's more of a man than I ever recognized, powerful and in control. With the scent of his musk covering my skin, combined with his clean masculine cologne, I'm lost in his aroma. It's more than that. Perhaps it's because I'm naked, and he just fucked my mouth. Maybe it's because he's still mostly dressed, except for his cock, which is again standing to attention. No matter the cause, I'm fascinated by his presence.

He rubs my jaw joint, kisses my forehead, and asks, "What do you say? I just removed the gag."

"Thank you, Sir." There it is again, that tone I barely recognize. Even so, I can't believe how freely the words flow.

In the bathroom, he turns on the water and waits as it warms. Out of habit, I try to look in the mirror, but his presence blocks me. I can't see what I look like. I can't see if I've changed. Yet somehow I feel different.

As the water warms, he uncuffs my wrists, allowing my hands to fall to my side. I feel his gaze on my skin—every inch of it—watching my every move. Steam begins to fill the room when Victor speaks, his voice rumbling through me, like thunder through the mist. "Undress me."

I don't hesitate as I lift his T-shirt over his head. It had been tight enough to showcase that his body is trim and fit, but without it I see the definition in his abs. I resist the urge to touch him and instead, kneel to remove his shoes and socks. Once he's kicked off his jeans, and I'm still on the ground, I look up. "Sir, I can suck you much better without that thing in my mouth."

With an angry expression, Victor lifts me by the shoulders—as if I weigh nothing—and his tone is harsh. "No topping from the bottom, kitten. I'm in control."

My insides clench at his words. He's right. I was trying to take charge. "I'm sorry, Sir."

Not acknowledging my apology, he directs my moves. "In the shower."

With my head hung in shame, I step behind the curtain. The warm water falls down, flattening my hair and filling the small space with the aroma of wet hairspray. For a moment, I worry about the makeup, the mascara that must be dark streaks, creating rivers running down my cheeks. And then I realize how much I've cried since we left the TV station and the way Victor's seed showered me—my face, my boobs, and my body. More than likely, I already have raccoon eyes and dark streaks down my cheeks.

I exhale as Sir suds a cloth and gently cleans my face. Instructing me to face the wall with my hands upon the tile, slowly, methodically, he washes my hair and body. Up my thighs, cleaning away not only the evidence of his arousal but my own as well. I moan as he washes near the belt.

"It's your punishment for lying," he says.

I lower my chin. "I'm sorry."

"Tell me what you lied about."

"About wanting your cock." Tears again prickle my eyes. "It's just wrong. I shouldn't want it, not like this."

He brushes his finger along the edge of the belt, close, but unable to reach where I need him. I writhe, wanting him closer, needing him inside me.

"Does it feel wrong?"

His hands move to my breasts, cupping, kneading, and pinching. I push backward, searching for his hard dick, wanting it against me, wanting to feel it. It can't be inside me with the belt, but I can relish its hardness against my lower back as it pushes and probes.

My head moves backward with the tug of my wet hair. "Does it?"

"No, Sir. It doesn't feel wrong."

"I told you that I'd punish you for lying. Did you lie about your pussy wanting my cock?"

Again with the vulgar words. I swallow. "Yes, Sir. I did. I admitted I did."

"Then tell me how I'm punishing you, what I'm doing to you."

"Now," I answer, "you're not letting me have it, nor are you touching me where I need you to."

"Do you want me to touch you?"

My mind surrenders as my body electrifies. The droplets of water falling upon my skin are needles prickling my flesh. My Sir's voice is thunder. His hands are salvation. Only through him can I find relief. "Yes," I admit.

He spins me around and lifts my chin. His eyes are black, his pupils dilated, only small brown circles like outlines. "Yes...?"

"Yes, Sir. I want you to touch me."

"So you lied."

"I'm ashamed."

"We have all weekend, kitten. Here's your choice: either you keep the chastity belt on until tomorrow morning or you choose to take another form of punishment, and when I'm done with that, I'll fuck your needy cunt. The choice is yours."

Chapter 8

VICTOR

My Erika's nipples bead at the prospect and my use of words I've never before used in her presence. They make her uncomfortable...no, the fact that she likes it makes her uncomfortable. Her body quakes under my grasp as I turn off the water and reach for a towel. "What will it be, kitten?"

She's so much prettier without all the stage makeup. Her skin is fresh and pink from the warm water. Her eyes are clear and lips are red and swollen from the gag. She's a vision, and more importantly, she's mine.

"What other punishment?" she asks as I dry her, inch by inch, caressing her skin. The indecision in her voice is loud and clear, even to the untrained ear. Erika saw the cross and the various implements. She has an idea of what my plans could include.

"Trust. Obedience. Submission. Your punishment is for me to decide," I explain. "Your choice is something else. I'll either take off the chastity belt or I won't. If I don't, wearing it is your punishment. That means no fucking until tomorrow. No having my cock inside of you. No having my tongue or fingers in your greedy wet pussy or your tight hole."

Her blue eyes shine with desire and apprehension, but she doesn't speak.

"Before you decide..." I offer, knowing this is all new to her. "...I'll show you something."

Though her light brown hair is still wet, her skin is dry, except for where water drips from her long tresses. We're both naked as I lead her back to the big room and to the bondage table.

"What is this?" she asks as she runs the palm of her hand over the soft vinyl surface.

"Husband," I say.

Kitten looks from me to the bondage table and repeats what I said. Her word is more of a question. "Husband?"

"It's your safe word."

A turmoil of emotions swirls in her blue eyes with

knowledge of her powerful word. Will that word make her realize that she's supposed to be with me? Or will she use that word and go back to a life of safety and boredom?

Kitten nods. "Okay."

"Do you know what that means?"

"If I say it, you'll stop."

"It will *all* stop."

She nods again.

"Lie back on this part." I direct her to the broad vinyl-covered surface and help her recline. Placing her feet on the footrests, I decide not to bind her. "I'm not going to restrain you. A much more binding restraint is your mind. Close your eyes and decide what your future holds."

Though she isn't sure what I mean, she obeys. Closing her eyes and resting her arms on the attached rests, she opens her body to me.

"Don't fight me, kitten," I say, taking a crop from the wall and gently running it over her warm skin, beginning at her shoulder. Erika flinches at the first touch, but doesn't move away. Instead of striking, I trace the leather over her tits and around each nipple. The leather loop leaves a trail of goose flesh as it explores the intricacies of her toned body. She's perfect. Her job requires her to stay fit, but having her laid out in front of me, I see all of her. She's a masterpiece. I continue to trace the sexiness of her collarbone, the swell of her tits, and the flatness of her stomach. With each touch, her legs open wider. I marvel at how it's happening without my words, as only the crop teases the edge of the chastity belt.

The insides of her thighs quake as I continue to touch and torment. So close, yet unable to give her the relief she craves. Over and over I tease, only her breath filling the air until she yells.

"Something else!" Her words are filled with need.

Slap! The crop strikes her stomach, leaving an angry red welt.

"Sir," I correct.

Immediately her head bobs, and she says, "Something else, *Sir.*" The wanton desire is subdued as her now respectful tone fills the air, and a stream of tears leaks from the corners of her eyes.

"You want another punishment instead of the belt?"

"Yes. Please, Sir, punish me another way. This is too hard."

"Tell me why."

"Because I need your cock, Sir."

I bend down and lick away the tears brought on by the crop, savoring the salty taste. "Open your eyes and stand up." I offer her my hand.

Once she's standing, I go to the armoire and retrieve the key. Erika keeps her eyes downcast as I move closer, unlock the belt, and pull it from between her legs. "Look how wet this is."

Her gaze flutters to the belt, the crotch moist with her cum, and looks back to my feet.

"Why is that?" I ask.

"Because I want you, I need you, Sir."

"On the bed."

Without hesitation, my kitten crawls onto the mattress.

"I'm going to bind your hands. Once I do, I'm going to punish you, just like you asked for, and then I'm going to fuck you. Do you remember your safe word?"

"Yes, Sir."

She lies near the top of the bed and lifts her hands over her head. As she gets into position, I marvel at her beauty. She's the most magnificent woman in the world. She always has been. I've never wanted anyone else. Now, with her hands bound together and secured to the headboard, she's perfection. "You're mine," I remind her, petting her soft skin. "You always will be."

Erika doesn't speak, but with her hands above her head, her hips wiggle, responding to my touch and words.

"Roll over. I want your ass in the air."

It's not easy with her hands bound, but diligently she tries.

As Erika struggles to comply, I contemplate my choices of implements for pleasure and pain. This is all new to her. She isn't ready for a cane or even a whip. I run a few of the paddles over my hand. Some are long and rectangular, reminding me of a fraternity board, while others are covered in leather, and some are both with holes. I take one of the leather ones, shaped much like a ping-pong paddle complete with a peppering of holes, and go back to the bed.

"This will do." I strike the paddle against my hand and let the combination of my words and the sound sink in.

In her position, my kitten's unable to see what I selected. The possibilities must be replaying in her pretty mind. Stillness descends over the cabin, and I notice how her body quakes. I wonder what she must be thinking, being out of control, being at my mercy. I can only assume it's a staggering concoction of anticipation, want, and fear. The evidence of her desire is visible on her thighs. The intoxicating aroma of her cum and emotions fills the room, causing her to squirm against the bindings. She gasps as, without warning, I climb onto the bed and rub my hand over her round ass.

"You have a fucking gorgeous ass."

Over and over, I caress and warm her skin. I keep going, occasionally brushing her wet pussy until her head drops, her unrestrained hair falls over her face, and she moans in pleasure. Just as she does, I rear the paddle back and strike her ass.

"Fuck!" she screams.

My arm vibrates as her entire body shudders. Small white circles protrude like polka dots on her ass in the pattern of the paddle's holes. I can't resist touching them. When I do, she flinches. "Hold still, kitten. This is what you chose. Remember?"

"I-I didn't..." She stops her own rebuttal. "Yes, Sir."

I don't back down as again I strike her ass, letting the leather paddle redden her skin, creating a pattern of pink and red circles. Her breath hitches as she gives in to the pain. Her curses turn to whimpers as more tears flow.

After a few more blows, she falls forward, collapsing with a muffled scream. "Stop."

I lean down with my lips near her ear and my most menacing tone. "That's not your safe word. Either say it, or get back on your elbows and knees and don't fall again. If you do, you'll only increase your punishment."

I wait for her to respond. When she doesn't, I stick out my tongue and lap her newest tears. She sucks in a deep breath. I kiss her cheek as any rebuttals she may have considered fade away, and on shaky limbs she moves back into position. One more kiss to her cheek and her muscles relax, ready to take what I choose to give her.

Smack!

"Thank me."

Her voice trembles. "Thank you, Sir."

I reel back and strike again.

"T-thank you, Sir."

Between her acknowledgments, cries, and the reddening of her ass, my cock is rock hard and the tip is glistening with cum.

"That's it, kitten, scream, cry—just don't move

from your position. No one can hear your apprecia-
tion of your punishment except me. That's why
we're here."

Smack!

"T-thank you, Sir." Her words are barely audible.

"Why am I doing this?" I ask.

Smack!

"Thank you. I-I didn't tell y-you the truth, Sir."
It's difficult for her to speak through her sobs.

With each strike, her thighs become more and
more wet. By the time both of her ass cheeks are fire-
engine red, her thighs are slick, and her face is
covered with tears.

Chapter 9
ERIKA

Fuck!

My ass is on fire. I've never felt anything like this before. But even so, I refuse to use my safe word. If I do, I'm afraid he'll stop. Not just the punishment—I'm ready for that to stop—but what's coming next. I need Victor inside me. I've never been more turned on in my entire life.

I wait for the next strike. How many have there been? I don't know. The cabin echoes with our breaths, my whimpers, and the sound of my blood rushing through my veins. I try to breathe, but my nose is running and my lungs won't work. There are so many sensations, but all I concentrate on is keeping my position and repeating my gratitude, even though my arms and legs are shaking.

When another strike doesn't happen, I wonder if it's over. Did I do it? Did I survive my Sir's punishment? Can I collapse? I want to collapse.

The paddle hits the ground, its sound the final bell letting me know I made it. I gasp as Victor spreads my overly sensitive ass cheeks and his tongue laps at my core. Despite the pain from him holding me, I can't contain the groan as I push my ass toward him, wanting his tongue deeper. After the punishment he delivered, I can't comprehend words adequate to describe the pleasure his tongue is giving me. My knees and elbows shake as he licks and laps at my essence.

"Roll over."

His deep voice is all I hear.

My body and mind are no longer connected, but are two separate entities.

My mind is saying that this is wrong. It's telling me to scream my safe word—husband—and make it all end. My body, however, is strung tighter than it's ever been. My insides have never felt as empty, never needed a man more than I need Victor Cross, and never been this wet or wanting.

My body wins as I fumble for the binding holding my wrists and turn, rolling onto my back.

"Shit," I mumble as my ass hits the comforter, the rough material biting into my freshly punished skin. Why wasn't I honest? He told me to be honest. The bed shifts with his weight.

"Open your eyes."

I hadn't even realized they were closed when I open them. Right in front of me, kneeling between my unashamedly spread legs, is Victor. The length of his cock is in his hand as he strokes the tightly stretched skin. The tip shines with pre-cum, and I imagine sucking it with my lips, bringing him pleasure, more than he could have had with that gag.

"Tell me, kitten, what do you want?"

"Your cock, Sir." The words come too easily. I lift my knees higher, giving him my pussy, presenting it to him. It's his and after this, it always will be.

Leaning toward me, his weight on his forearms on either side of my face, Victor stares deep into my eyes, silently daring me to speak, to say my safe word.

I can't.

I can't do anything but look back into his dark eyes, and then I remember to look away, to submit to his desire. When I do, when my lids lower in reverence to this man, a moan comes from my throat. More sounds that I've never heard spill from my lips as Sir enters me, filling me, stretching me. It's for his pleasure, but it's mine too. With each thrust he pushes me toward the headboard. I try to lift my throbbing ass, but I can't, not with the way he's taking me, ravaging me, ruthlessly pounding into me. The pain and pleasure mount, piling one on top of the other as energy flows through me, curling my toes and causing my fingernails to bite into the palms of my hands. After only a few deep and savage thrusts, my body comes undone.

Fireworks ignite behind my partially closed eyes. I scream, but I don't know what I'm saying. The world is out of kilter, or maybe it's finally right. Victor doesn't stop or even slow to allow me to enjoy the downside of my orgasm. He continues to fuck, brutally pounding. He isn't pleasing me, though I've never been so pleased. This is about him, about his pleasure. The realization propels me back up the figurative mountain until my body tenses and we both come undone.

He grunts as he fills me with his seed, over and over, combining it with my essence until I'm overflowing. It doesn't end there. He turns me, twisting me in positions I've never known. Each time, his cock finds the exact spot to send me over the edge. I don't know how many times he uses me, how many times I come, or even how many ways. But by the time I fall asleep, I know without a doubt that he's marked me in a way I've never been marked. I know I can't go back to what I had before.

When I wake, my arms are no longer bound. Instead, I'm draped over Victor, or the man I now call *Sir*. I'm not sure I can ever call him Master, but I never thought *Sir* would be in my vocabulary either. My cheek is lying upon his solid chest, and his strong arm is wrapped protectively around my shoulder. Despite the aches throughout my body, I've never felt more satisfied or safer than I do at this moment.

I raise my head, push my hair away, and look at his features. His narrow nose, chiseled jaw with a day's beard growth. How had I not noticed how handsome he is?

His dark brown eyes open and a slight grin comes to his lips. I lower my lids, knowing that seeing him smile fills me with relief and delight I never imagined. I want him to be happy.

"Good morning, kitten."

His voice is like thunder on my newly awakened ears. It rumbles through me, bringing my nervous system back to life with a jolt of lightning. I start to pull away, not because I want to, but because my bladder is full.

Sir's large hand grasps my arm, stopping my escape.

It's then I realize that I didn't answer. "Good morning, Sir."

"Where do you think you're going?"

His menacing tone and tightening grip have my body on a virtual treadmill. I'm running a six-minute mile. My heart rate accelerates as my skin peppers with goose flesh from the flood of heat within.

I look up. "I-I was..." Again, my lids lower and I let out a breath. "Sir, may I use the bathroom?"

He releases my arm and slaps my tender ass.

"Hurry, and no pleasuring yourself. If you do, I won't do it when you get back."

My cheeks heat and rise as I scurry to the edge of the bed. This is all so new and so different. When was the last time I asked permission for something so basic?

As I walk, my entire body aches with the aftereffects of his punishment and the multiple rounds of fucking. I'm not sure which one caused the most ache. All I know is that the more he gives, the more I want —of either, of both.

When I make my way out of the bathroom, my steps stutter as I take him in. He's so sexy, lying there. The sheet has moved, and his erection is standing at attention, his large hand moving slowly up and down his hard rod. As if he heard me, his dark eyes turn and drink me in. They're commanding me silently, telling me without words that I'm his. I take one step.

"No, crawl to me."

I don't hesitate as I drop to my hands and knees. The worn wood floor is smooth yet gritty as I move closer. Each movement taking me closer floods my core anew.

As I reach the side of the bed, my eyes are down. I want nothing more than to see him, to watch him as he does what he forbade me from doing.

The thunder rolls. "Kitten, do you want to stay down there on the floor?"

"No, Sir."

"Then get your ass up here."

I quickly climb onto the bed and hurry along the length of the mattress until I'm beside him.

Our gazes meet. Without a word Sir pulls me over him as if I'm as light as air and moves me so I'm straddling his torso. "I want your ass," he says, "but first, I want to watch you fuck me."

"Isn't that topping from the bottom?"

I jump as he swats my sore behind again. "It's not when I tell you to do it. Now, kitten, get on my cock and start moving. I want to watch your tits swing and feel your cunt strangle my dick."

My body electrifies at his voice, his words, and his commands. Lifting myself on my knees, I grasp his cock beneath me; my thumb and middle finger are unable to touch as I hold his girth. Lining the tip up with my entrance, I slowly begin to slide down, but before I can, Sir grabs my hips and roughly pulls me toward him.

"Shit," I say as I adjust to his size.

"Kitten, you're so fucking wet, I just slid right into your tight pussy."

I lower my eyes, knowing he is right.

He crosses his arms behind his head and grins. The muscles in his biceps become more defined as his cheeks rise. The view takes my breath away as his gaze devours me.

"Fuck me, kitten. When you're done, I'll let you cook me breakfast. If you make me come, I may even let you eat."

Tingles radiate from my head to my toes as my

knees begin to flex. The friction is phenomenal, but that isn't my goal. I don't concentrate on climbing my mountain. My only goal is assuring that he's satisfied. It's not because I'm worried about food—I know he won't let me starve. I want him to come because I want to please him more than I want sustenance.

It isn't until his back arches and neck strains that I let myself feel the burn. As he grips my hips again, I know we're going to come together. It's when he roars that I let loose, my insides milking his cock, encouraging his release, and wanting every last drop.

Chapter 10
VICTOR

I sit at the small table in my unbuttoned jeans as my kitten prepares my breakfast. I purposely supplied the cabin with foods I knew she wouldn't normally eat.

"Pancakes?" she asks, looking at the box.

"Pancakes."

"What will I eat?" Her bruised ass shows as she leans naked, searching the refrigerator.

"Pancakes."

She spins toward me, her lips parted to speak. I know what she normally eats for breakfast. There is no fruit or yogurt in the refrigerator. With its sparse contents, she knows that too. I watch as she fights her normal response to argue.

But this isn't normal. It is our future.

"B-but, Sir."

"Cook. And there's bacon too."

She pulls the container from the refrigerator. It's not the precooked kind. It will require her frying it. The way she's holding it—her cute little nose scrunched and eyes narrowed—you'd think it were trash in her hand, not uncooked meat.

"Kitten, I'm not repeating myself." I stand and walk toward her. Lifting the spatula from the counter, I tap it against my hand. "Tell me what you'll eat, or I'm spanking your ass." I turn it over, evaluating the pattern. "I bet this would make a great design on your skin."

Her blue eyes go from the bacon to the box of pancake mix and then to the spatula in my grasp. "Okay, pancakes and bacon, but no syrup."

My grin grows. "Oh, there will be syrup."

Leaving the spatula on the counter, I turn around and walk back to the table. As I do, I hear the rattling of bowls and pans. Without another word, she does as she's been told. Watching her cook for me, naked, is sexy in a way I never imagined.

As the cabin fills with the delicious aroma of pancakes and frying bacon, her concentration zeros in on the cast-iron skillet. I never thought about the popping and crackling grease with bare skin, but it's obvious, at this moment, it's my kitten's number-one concern.

Once she's compiled a plate of pancakes and another of bacon, she brings them to the table. She brings me a plate and silverware before refilling my cup of coffee.

So far, she hasn't even had coffee. I'm making her wait.

It's as she reaches for the second plate that I stop her. "Just the syrup. No other plate is necessary."

"But you said..." My kitten stops herself before she says more.

I reach for the bottle of syrup and point to the floor. Spreading my legs, I wait as the indecision clouds her beautiful eyes.

"Trust, obey, submit," I remind her.

Slowly, she falls to her knees and crawls to the area between my legs. "Here," I say as I bring my coffee cup to her lips. The liquid has cooled to the perfect warmth. She practically hums as I tilt the cup for her to drink.

When she's finished drinking, I open my eyes wide.

"Thank you, Sir," she says as she lowers hers.

Right in front of her is my erection. If I'd taken medicine to help with an erection—which I didn't—according to the commercial, I'd need to call a doctor. I've been fucking hard since she got in my truck.

I remove two pancakes and cover them in syrup. I know this is pushing her limits. That's why I didn't leave it to her to eat on her own. "Open your mouth, kitten. Close your eyes."

Her breasts heave as she does as I command. As the sticky, sweet cake gets to her lips, she closes them tight, blocking the way.

"Kitten."

"Please, Sir," she mumbles through closed lips.

I'm not going to entertain her concerns. She's beautiful. She's perfect. Her body needs more than fruit and vegetables to sustain her this weekend.

When I don't speak, simply setting my jaw and narrowing my eyes, she peers my way and acquiesces. Her lips part. As the syrup-covered pancake lands on her tongue, she sighs.

"Chew and swallow." After she does, I ask, "How does it taste?"

"Oh my God, it's delicious."

"Come here." I pat my leg and she climbs up onto my lap.

Our breakfast is consumed from one another's lips, her feeding me and me doing the same. Syrup drips from her chin to her breasts where I lick it off her skin. By the time we're done, she's eaten not only at least two of the pancakes but also two full strips of bacon.

I can't take having her sexy naked body on my lap any longer without taking her again. Directing her to lie on the floor, I then reach for the bottle of syrup and stand above her.

"Vic—Sir?"

"Oh, kitten, I want to be sure your memories of this weekend *stick*."

At my words, her face blossoms into the sweetest —no pun intended—smile. Her hair is a sex-tangled halo, and she's not wearing any makeup. Her eyes sparkle, cheeks grow pink, and her lips shine with syrup. It's not at all like the Erika the world sees on TV. The vision before me is sincere and real and more stunning than she's ever been onscreen.

I smile as Erika struggles to stay still as I drizzle syrup over her tits and stomach. Though I might have considered punishing her to watch her skin again turn red, I can't. I need to be inside her.

Stepping out of my jeans, I kneel between her spread legs and look down at the sticky concoction flowing over her light skin. "You're beautiful."

She doesn't speak as her lids flutter and she veils her eyes.

"No, kitten, look at me."

Her blue eyes grow wide as she takes in my naked form.

"I'm going to fuck you again. And then, after we shower, I'm going to do it again and again. What do you have to say about that?"

"Thank you, Sir."

My grin quirks upward as I take my syrup-covered fingers and tease her swollen clit. Her hips writhe at my touch as she squirms on the tile floor. I lower my chest until we're plastered together and my cock teases her entrance.

"What do you want?"

"If I lie, will you punish me?"

"Yes."

"If I tell the truth, will you fuck me and then punish me?"

I swear my cock doubles in size. "I could punish you for topping from the bottom."

Erika nods. "Please fuck me first. I want you."

"And then?"

"I suppose that's up to you."

I narrow my eyes.

"Sir," she adds in the sweetest tone.

I couldn't do anything else but comply: my need is too great. I push inside her warm haven. As I do, her back arches and her syrup-covered breasts push upward. My thrusts still as I lap my finger in the syrup and bring it to her lips. "Open."

She doesn't hesitate as she takes my finger between her lips. Her tongue teases as she licks.

"Fuck."

I remove my finger and resume our rhythm. In and out, the sensation of her walls surrounding me—squeezing me—with no condom separating us is heaven. I always knew it would be.

When we both come, I stay inside her, my body stuck to hers as I support myself on my elbow. I can't take my eyes off her. She's all I've ever wanted. The expression of bliss on her beautiful face is better than anything I've ever seen.

I tuck a piece of her gorgeous hair behind her ear

and smile. "Kitten, you realize we aren't using birth control?"

"Yes. And it feels so good."

"You could get pregnant with my baby."

She nods. "It's what you want."

"It is," I confirm. "What do you want?"

Her sexy body wiggles beneath mine. "To be with you, forever."

"I love you, kitten."

She lifts her gaze until our eyes meet. "I've always loved you, Vic."

Chapter 11

VICTOR

"Hmm," Dr. Kizer says with a smile as we walk into her office, hand in hand.

Erika's cheeks redden as she leans against my shoulder.

"Dr. Kizer," I say in greeting.

The counselor's smile broadens. "Tell me, Mr. Cross, Ms. Ellis: how was the cabin?"

I squeeze Erika's hand. "I think it was just what the doctor ordered."

"Ms. Ellis?" the counselor asks.

"Erika *Cross*, Mrs. Victor Cross," my wife says. "I'm having them change my name at the station too. Soon it will be Erika Cross on channel fifty-three. I had some preconceived notion that I couldn't advance in my career if I used my married name, but now I realize what that did to Vic. We've been married for almost five years; I want everyone to know."

"Victor," Dr. Kizer asks, "how do you feel about that?"

"I think I have the only woman I've ever loved next to me at this moment."

Dr. Kizer nods. "My fee includes use of the cabin. If you two are all done there, we can adjust—"

"No," Erika and I say together. Though a smile tugs at my lips, I narrow my eyes at my wife in an unspoken warning.

Her blue eyes sparkle as she lowers her lids. "I'm sorry, Sir. It's your decision."

"Doctor, we'd like to use the cabin again next weekend."

She grins. "Very good. I admit it's an unconventional therapy, but for some it's exactly what's needed."

Erika's cheeks grow pink, and I recall how red her ass was with the paddle. "It was."

"Erika, tell me how you felt when Victor took you there."

She sighs as she looks at me and back at our counselor. "Scared, excited, confused."

"Go on."

"Happy and so fulfilled."

"Can you explain?"

Erika's light pink lips disappear for a moment behind her teeth as her blue eyes glisten. "I thought we were done—that our marriage was over. I didn't think there was enough energy or desire on either of our parts. I can't tell you how much it means to me to know that Victor loves me enough to plan all of that, to push me out of our normal, and..." Her voice cracks. "...reignite the sparks that I thought had died."

Dr. Kizer tilts her head. "The way he took you to the cabin was also unconventional. What do you have to say about that?"

Erika looks from the counselor to me and back. "I've thought a lot about it. As it was happening, I was scared. I was afraid he'd gone mad..."

"And then?"

My wife's smile broadens. "He was right to do it that way. If he would have asked me to go, explained his plan, I would have said no. I would have over-thought the whole thing and let rational reasoning rule."

"And then?"

Erika squeezes my hand. "I don't want to think about it. I'm afraid our marriage would be over."

"What about you, Victor?" Dr. Kizer asks.

I swallow the lump growing in my throat. I'm the Dom in this relationship, yet the truth is that I'd do anything for the woman beside me. "I was excited and to be honest, nervous. I'd talked the whole plan up in my head and believed it was the right way to go." I turn to Erika's trusting blue eyes. "Yet I know Erika, and she can be stubborn."

Erika smiles.

"It wasn't until I pulled the truck over onto the side of the road and learned how aroused she was that I knew we still had a chance."

Dr. Kizer leans back against her chair and looks from me to Erika and back. "Well, it sounds like the cabin was a good start. It's yours for as long as you need it. I'm sure you still have a few things yet to explore."

"Yes, we do." I grin at Erika as her cheeks grow even rosier. We never made it to the canes, nor did I take her ass. Everything that we did do was a lot for our first time as Dom and sub. Though Erika may have questioned it once or twice during our weekend, I wanted her to be comfortable.

"My advice," the counselor says, "use the cabin. Fan those flames. But don't forget to talk. Communication is the key to keeping that flame alive.

"Erika, was the name change your idea?"

My wife looks up. "It was. Vic didn't even ask me to do it. I wanted to. I never realized how important my taking his last name was to him—and to me." She adds, "I want the world to know that I'm his."

"Victor?"

"I'd brand my fucking name on her forehead, but this will work."

Chapter 12

ERIKA

"Oh, Sir!"

The lights of the cabin are low as Victor's cock teases my core, rubbing over my clit and moving in and out of my entrance. I can't hear anything but his voice, his breathing, the slaps of the flogger still ringing in my ears.

"Please," I beg. My voice cracks with need, wanting him deeper, wanting more.

"I told you, kitten, where I was going to fuck you, and it's not in this tight, warm pussy."

My throat dries as I try to swallow. I've gone along with everything since last weekend. And while Victor made me nervous on our first drive to the cabin, everything since has been as he promised. It's my fantasies played out in real life. Over the last week, after our appointment with Dr. Kizer, we've taken the time to talk to one another. We've been honest and said things we should have said long before. More than that, these new roles have given our marriage something we've never had—total trust and freedom.

Freedom to be open with one another with our bodies and our hearts. Freedom to give the kind of trust and submission it takes to allow a person to do what Victor has done and is doing to me. My wrists are bound to the bondage table, but instead of lying flat, my ankles are also bound, attached with short chains that hook to my wrists. I'm on my knees and shoulders with my cheek pressed to the table and my ass in the air. I couldn't straighten my legs if I wanted to.

His finger moves in and out of me. Each time it's gone, I tremble at the loss. Not only that, but each time it leaves me, it gets closer and closer to my tight hole. I'm scared, but by the evidence on my husband's fingers, I'm also excited.

"Do you trust me, kitten?"

"Yes, I do, Sir." My answer gives me the strength to let him continue. Though I can't believe this is going to happen after years of protest, I'm equally as excited. This is what he's wanted since we were first married, but for the first time, it's also what I want.

I shiver as cold gel combines with my essence as Victor lubricates my tight ring of muscles.

"When you get used to this," he explains, "we won't need the gel. You're always so fucking wet. But now, I want to make it easy. I don't want to hurt you."

His words seem ironic, being as he's just flogged my ass and thighs. Unlike a paddle, the flogger has an array of leather pieces, their ends like sharp whips as they abraded my skin. Though they never cut, it felt as though they did.

Each strike wasn't one, but twenty as the flogger reddened my ass and thighs. Nevertheless, I understand what Vic means. I understand the difference between intentional pain for pleasure and pain for harm. My husband chose the flogger to clear my mind, to get me ready, and bring my focus on him, where it belongs.

It worked. Not only because of the pain, but because I trust him to know how much I can take. Because I do trust, I'll also obey and submit. Now, my mind is clear. Nothing else exists beyond the walls of this cabin.

I whimper as his finger penetrates the tight ring of muscle.

"Kitten, listen to my voice."

I do. My mind slides into that space where I'm filled with the deep timbre.

"Yes, Sir."

"Do it. Trust me."

The flogging left my ass and thighs tingling while building my want. I long for relief. I take a deep breath, close my eyes, and concentrate on his movements—the way his finger moves in and out of my ass and the way his other hand works my clit. He knows my body better than I do. Just as with the punishment, he knows exactly how much I can take.

Higher and higher he strums me until my toes curl.

"Not yet."

I hold my breath as the tip of his cock presses against me.

"Relax and I'll let you come."

I've learned his meanings. He is really saying that if I don't relax, he won't let me come. And as much as I want air right now, I want to experience an orgasm. In the last week, we've had more sex than in the last two years. It's left me sore and wanton. Each time shows me how good it can be, making me desire more of what only Vic can do.

There's no more self-gratification after an erotic read. I am allowed to read the novels, but Sir wants me to read them aloud. If I thought they were sexy reading them to myself, I had no idea what it would be like to read as he teases my skin, making me hot and bothered.

"Who owns you, kitten? Who do you belong to?"

"To you, Sir."

"And what do you want?" His cock pushes harder, applying more pressure.

I push back toward him as much as I can in my bindings. "To come. Please, Sir, fuck my ass and let me come."

He'd told me before that he wouldn't take my ass until I begged. I never thought I would, but I just did. I'd do anything for him.

I suck in a breath and ball my fists as he plunges forward, taking my ass and making it his. Tears leak to the table as he moves; thrust after thrust, the fire inside me burns until the rhythm is right, and my body accepts the invasion. His warmth covers my freshly punished skin. My thoughts are monopolized by the fiery burn of his cock in my ass and pleasure of his fingers on my clit.

Higher and tighter I go, lost in the sound of his breathing until I see explosions of light, and I come apart. Moments later Victor does too, filling me with his seed until I'm overflowing.

He pulls out and kisses my most private parts. Next he unfastens the chains and my legs relax. When he rolls me over, his expression takes my breath away. So much love and adoration. He smooths back my hair, tucking a piece behind my ear, and gently kisses my lips.

"Kitten, you're perfect and you're mine —forever."

I'm too tired to speak. Instead, I smile and nod. He's right.

I am.

This may seem unconventional to others. I'm not sure I can tell even Jenn what we've been doing. She already knows that my attitude has changed. It is impossible to hide my satisfied grin when I mention his name.

He's my husband, my love, my life, and my Sir.

Chapter 13

VICTOR

A year later

I lean against the studio wall with my arms crossed over my chest as I watch the stagehands unplug my beautiful wife from her microphone. It's a good thing they're disconnecting her because a hot mic might not be a good idea with what I have planned for us back in her dressing room.

"Let me help you, Mrs. Cross," Erika's assistant, Abby, says as she offers Erika her hand.

My laughter fills the emptying set as Erika kicks off her shoes and lets Abby help her stand. At nearly eight and a half months pregnant, she's made no bones about her hatred of the fucking heels. While I can understand her discomfort, I admit that imagining her and nothing but four-inch heels makes my boxer briefs strain under my trousers—even with her ever-growing midsection.

If I think about it too much, it'll be obvious to everyone.

She didn't become pregnant immediately after we stopped using birth control. Though I'd been the one to first mention children, it was she who was concerned. She even contacted her doctor. He assured us that everything was working; we just needed time. I'll never forget her tears of joy as the small plus sign appeared.

Heels in hand, Erika walks my direction. I can't describe how beautiful she is. Even with the heavy makeup and her hair styled to perfection, I'm in awe. You'd think those would be the standout attributes, but they're far down the list compared to her natural beauty.

Her cheeks pinken as her eyelids flutter.

Erika Cross of *The Cross Report*, her very own cable network news program, is kick-ass in every way. She can banter and discuss facts with the best and the brightest. Her natural wit, immense knowledge, and common sense are only surpassed by her determination. That's the hard-core newswoman the world sees.

She's the one who not long after our first trip to the cabin was contacted about her dream job: her own cable news program, filming live five days a week from New York. The offer was her ambition come to pass; she deserves it for her hard work. As her biggest fan, I wouldn't have wanted anything less. We were both elated.

Now, as the distance between us lessens and her smile grows, her eyes move to downcast. This is the Erika that only I see: the incredibly sensual, ravishing submissive. The love of my life who's found the balance she needs in leading her colleagues while allowing only me to dominate her.

I won't lie. Watching her call some politician or spokesperson on the carpet with her fiery comebacks and well-researched responses is as much of a turn-on as her naked body bound to our four-poster bed and her skin marked from my newest purchase. Currently, in her condition, I am willing to turn it down a notch or two.

She is the one who continues to push for more, assuring me that our baby wants Mommy and Daddy satisfied.

Yes, I'm aware she's topping from the bottom. It's just another excuse to punish her sexy-as-shit round ass.

"Sir," she whispers as she leans toward me for a kiss.

After our lips touch, I lift her chin until her blue

gaze is captured by mine. "Excellent show, Mrs. Cross."

Her cheeks rise. "Thank you, Sir. I'm not sure the current White House spokesperson is as pleased."

I chuckle. "You kicked his ass. The tape of his testimony during the judiciary committee hearing was genius."

"I'm glad it worked. It was a gamble." She lets out a long sigh. "Thank goodness, it's the weekend. I'm ready to leave *The Cross Report* behind for a couple of days."

I know that isn't one hundred percent accurate. She will read and research and do what she does, but first I plan to remind her who her first priority is.

I reach for her hand and give her a kiss on the forehead. "The studio always clears out quickly on Fridays. I have a surprise for you in your dressing room."

Her eyes sparkle in anticipation. "I'm intrigued."

Taking her shoes from her, we walk hand in hand down the narrow hallways until we reach the room with the nameplate *Erika Cross* on the door.

She lifts her fingers and runs them over the embossed sign. "I'm so sorry."

"Why?"

"I never meant to hurt you. That ridiculous notion about my name was obviously a misconception, a problem only in my head." She sighs and leans against the wall. "I can't even fathom all the changes since..." Her cheeks resume their signature pink as she runs her hands over our growing unborn baby. "...Dr. Kizer's unconventional therapy."

I lean down and kiss her midsection. When I straighten, Erika's expression is a glowing combination of love and respect with a sprinkling of exhaustion. "Kitten, I told you how incredible you were and are. I think maybe it took you relaxing without constantly worrying about every calorie or every inch of your skirt length to show the world what a talented firecracker of a debater you could be."

Her eyelids lower. "Thank you, Sir, for showing me what I need."

I tilt my head toward her door. "Inside, kitten, I've waited long enough."

With just a small change to my tone, the tension between us rises. Like an electric power surge, Erika's body tingles, her arousal emanating like a cloud.

She opens the door and looks around for my surprise. The large mirror with the chair for her makeup is exactly the same as usual. The sofa and table with fresh flowers is the same. At the far end is her desk. She has a bigger one in another office down the hall. Truth be told, as her manager—no longer one of the camera crew—I use the one in here more than she does.

"I don't see—"

I stop her words, not with other words, or even a finger to her pert, luscious lips. It's simply a stance and a glance. Seeing my feet apart, chin lifted, and eyes narrowed, Erika Cross becomes silent.

It's a trick I could share with her guests, but I don't want to. She's only mine to silence.

Her head falls forward as she lowers herself to her knees.

"Kitten, we have dinner plans. Remember that Jenn and Paul are in town?"

"Yes, Sir." She peers through her false eyelashes.

"But first, we're going to have some fun. Today's show was fantastic, but you need to clear your mind."

"Yes, Sir."

"Take me out, kitten."

I haven't used that spider mask since the first night in the cabin. It feels too good to feel Erika's lips on my hard cock.

I groan as she makes quick work of my belt, button, and zipper. I nod as she lowers my trousers and reaches for the waist band on my boxer briefs. "I plan to sit at dinner tonight knowing that your red lipstick is decorating my dick. Suck me."

Her entire body trembles as she opens her lips and leans forward.

Sometimes I fuck her mouth, but today, I'm giving her the pleasure of sucking me, allowing her to work me, leaving her red lipstick on my hard rod.

Just before I come, I stop her. "Over to the mirror, gorgeous."

I give her my hand and help her stand as she obeys my directions. "Show me those growing tits."

With a slight grin, she reaches back and unzips the top of her dress. Next she reaches for the snaps to her bra and unfastens them. As she eases out her arms, her luscious tits fall from their binding, heavy with need and growth. After kissing each one, I fall down to my knees and reach under the skirt to remove her panties. Once she steps out, I bring them to my nose.

"So wet. Are you a dirty slut?"

"Only for you, Sir."

"Hands on the counter."

She turns and leans forward, spreading her legs to shoulder-width apart. With our growing baby, this is a great position to fuck her from behind. That's what I plan to do. I'm not taking her ass right now. This is about helping her relax.

I lift the skirt of her dress, leaving it bunched around her waist. Finding her folds, I dip two fingers that slide into place as her essence coats my fingers. It's just as I predicted, warm and wet, clenching my digits like a vise as a moan escapes her lips and her legs stiffen.

Smack!

"Oh!"

"Did I say you could come?"

Smack!

"No, Sir." Her body trembles as she fights the war within her.

Since she became pregnant, her increased hormones have her libido on overdrive. I swear she can come while across the room with just the right look from me. Making her wait, taking her to the brink, and pulling her back teaches her patience as well as obedience.

I slap one side of her ass and then the other. "Look up, kitten. Look at the lust in your own eyes. You're fucking entrancing."

Smack!

I love watching her. The utter bliss as she slips away to that space where I'm her whole world. The day's tensions float away and her body melts, pliable to my will. It's like she's falling under a spell. Her blue eyes grow hazy as her ass grows red, decorated with my handprints.

Smack!

"Please, Sir," she begs in a whimper.

"Not yet." Two more quick slaps and I thrust inside her cunt.

"Oh!"

It's fucking heaven as she pushes back to my every thrust. In and out. Her growing tits swing in the mirror as my kitten becomes more and more lost to the sensations inside her. I wrap my arm around her, holding her upright. She's fighting her body's desire as her muscles grow tense. I keep moving as my other hand finds her clit.

"P-please..."

"Yes, kitten, come for me."

Her skin shimmers with a slick coating of perspiration as her head falls back, and she submits to the pleasure. Without my hold, she'd fall to the floor concentrating on nothing but her impending orgasm.

I hug her tighter against my chest, peppering her neck with kisses as we both come undone.

Still buried deep, I whisper, "If we were home, I'd have bound your hands to the ceiling."

She nods with a relaxed grin. "Thank you, Sir, for not letting me fall."

"Never, kitten. You're always safe with me."

Slowly I ease out, immediately missing her warmth. When I spin her around, I kiss her cheek. "Are you ready for dinner?"

"Or a nap."

I can't stop my smile. "Let's get you cleaned up, out of that stage makeup, and into something more comfortable." As I speak, our baby moves, pushing against Erika's stomach, stretching her skin that's leaning against my abdomen. I look down and smile. "I think our little one likes it when Mommy relaxes."

Erika shakes her head. "I was always so worried about gaining weight, and now look at me."

I reach behind her for her zipper and pull it down the rest of the way. Her dress slides to the floor, leaving her standing before me as she came into the world, as I plan to keep her most of the weekend. We're no longer in Wisconsin. The cabin is far away, but our apartment has been designed with a special room attached to our bedroom. It's our go-to place. There are no windows, no reminders of anyone but us. It's where the cares of the world disappear, lost to our desires.

"Kitten, you're stunning."

"If I disagree, will you punish me when we get home?"

I move my head back and forth as I watch my wife's lips quirk to a shy smile. "Topping from the bottom."

"I'm sorry, Sir. I need to be reminded."

I kiss her forehead. "Do you need help getting ready?"

"Yes, Sir."

The attached bathroom has a shower, but we don't have time for that. Instead, I warm the water in the sink as I douse a soft washcloth. Erika uses wipes to remove the bulk of the makeup while I add soap. "Same position, kitten."

Still nude, she places her hands on the counter as I gently wash away the evidence of our arousals. I'd love to use my tongue, but that wouldn't get us to dinner. Her ass is still red, though the raised skin has settled. I run the cloth over it, and she flinches. "It may be a little tender during dinner."

Erika's eyes meet mine in the mirror. "Good. It'll help me remember my priorities."

"I fucking love you."

"Thank you for loving me, for showing me what I need. I love you, too." She looks down to her midsection. "And our baby."

"And our baby."

Chapter 14

ERIKA

It is great to see Jenn and Paul. It's been nearly six months since I've seen my best friend, and they are only going to be in New York for a few days.

"Look at you!" Jenn shrieks as she reaches out to my swollen midsection and then wraps me in a hug.

When she backs up, she shakes her head.

"I know," I say. "I'm huge."

"No! You're absolutely radiant."

I shrug as I reach for Vic's arm. "I've never been happier."

"It shows," she says with a smile as she and Paul say their hellos to Vic.

Once we're seated at a very nice table, high above the city with a spectacular view of the city's lights, we all fall into easy conversation. That's the way it is with good friends—as if you've never been apart.

After our salads are finished, Jenn asks, "So you're really going to eat that filet you ordered?"

I smile as my gaze momentarily goes to my husband and then back to my best friend. "I am. The protein is good for the baby."

"Don't let her fool you," Vic says, "even before she was pregnant, she remembered her love of bacon."

"Bacon!" Jenn says, aghast.

"I still eat Greek salads and yogurt."

"I personally think it's great," Jenn says. "Like I said, you're simply radiant."

I notice how momentarily my friend's gaze goes to Paul and then back to her plate. There's something hauntingly familiar in her micro-expression.

"Jenn, I need to step away for a moment. Would you like to join me?"

She looks up from her plate. "Sure."

I give the two men my biggest smile. "We'll be right back. Babies and bladders—not the most comfortable combination." I turn to Vic. "Don't eat my steak."

Vic reaches for my hand and kisses my knuckles. "Hurry back."

"Yes..." I feel the warmth on my cheeks, knowing I almost called him *Sir* in front of our friends. By the twinkle in his dark eyes, he heard the unspoken title too.

Once Jenn and I are alone in the ladies' room, I turn to my friend. We don't have much time before our food arrives, and I don't want to miss the opportunity. "What's wrong?" I ask.

"Wrong?" she asks as her voice cracks and moisture fills her eyes.

"Oh, sweetheart," I coo as I wrap her shoulders in my arms. "Please talk to me."

Her head is shaking against my shoulder. "I wanted to talk to you. But every time I call, you sound so happy. I watch the show, and you look great. I don't want to be the one who brings you down." Her tear-filled eyes look at me. "I'm so happy for you. I remember not that long ago..."

The scene of the two of us in an empty restaurant replays in my head. "Is that it? Is it you and Paul?"

She nods. "I-I know I said we were good, and we were...until we weren't. There's been stress with his job and mine. Now...I'm afraid..."

My neck straightens. "Same questions you asked me: has he cheated?"

"No. I know he hasn't. I trust him."

"You?"

"No, never. I love him. It's just that..." Her head tilts. "How did you do it?"

"Do what?"

"How did you rekindle the spark? I can see it in your eyes and in Vic's. You look at Vic like's he your god."

"He is," I answer truthfully. "He's my everything. I'm not sure how much I can tell you."

Jenn grabs my hand. "Please. I want to save my marriage."

"Does Paul feel the same way?"

"I think so. This trip is supposed to be our time alone. I'm afraid it's too little, too late."

I squeeze her hand. "It's never too late. I thought it was for Vic and me, but I was wrong. I have the name of a marriage counselor back in Wisconsin. Would you be willing to explore some unconventional therapy?"

She shrugs. "I want to have what we had. No, I want what you have."

My mind momentarily goes to the remaining tingle in my ass. I'm not sure if she wants what I have or not, but I wouldn't change it for the world.

"Then go meet with Dr. Kizer. Let her get to know you. From what I understand, the route she recommended for us isn't her only therapy option. It may be right for you. It might not be. Be honest with her. Admit what's missing in your life. All I can say is that she couldn't have been more right for Vic and me."

"Please send me her information."

"I will. If you're honest with her, Paul, and yourself, you won't be sorry."

After drying Jenn's tears and my use of the facilities—our baby is camping out on my bladder—we go back to the table.

Vic stands as we approach. Leaning in, he kisses my cheek. "Is everything all right?"

"Everything is perfect, *Sir*." I whisper the last word.

Unconventional was our answer; maybe it will be for Jenn and Paul too.

Only time will tell.

More from Aleatha:

I hope you enjoyed my lighter side with a darker twist in UNCONVENTIONAL. For more of my works ranging from dark to light check out these links:

THE CONSEQUENCES SERIES: (bestselling dark romance)
(First in the series FREE)
https://www.aleatharomig.com/consequences-series

THE INFIDELITY SERIES: (acclaimed romantic saga)
(First in the series FREE)
https://www.aleatharomig.com/infidelity-series

INSIDIOUS (stand-alone smart, sexy thriller):
https://www.aleatharomig.com/insidious

THE LIGHT DUET: (romantic thriller series)
https://www.aleatharomig.com/light-series

ALEATHA'S LIGHTER ONES (stand-alone light, fun, and sexy romances guaranteed to leave you with a smile and maybe a tear)
https://www.aleatharomig.com/light-series

About the Author

Aleatha Romig is a New York Times, Wall Street Journal, and USA Today bestselling author who lives in Indiana, USA. She has raised three children with her high school sweetheart and husband of over thirty years. Before she became a full-time author, she worked days as a dental hygienist and spent her nights writing. Now, when she's not imagining mind-blowing twists and turns, she likes to spend her time with her family and friends. Her other pastimes include reading and creating heroes/anti-heroes who haunt your dreams!

Aleatha impresses with her versatility in writing. She released her first novel, CONSEQUENCES, in August of 2011. CONSEQUENCES, a dark romance, became a bestselling series with five novels and two companions released from 2011 through 2015. The compelling and epic story of Anthony and Claire Rawlings has graced more than half a million e-readers. Her first stand-alone smart, sexy thriller INSIDIOUS was next. Then Aleatha released the five-novel INFIDELITY series, a romantic suspense saga, that took the reading world by storm, the final book landing on three of the top bestseller lists. She ventured into traditional publishing with Thomas and Mercer. Her books INTO THE LIGHT and AWAY FROM THE DARK were published through this mystery/thriller publisher in 2016. In the spring of 2017, Aleatha again ventured into a different genre with her first fun and sexy stand-alone romantic comedy with the USA Today bestseller PLUS ONE.

Aleatha is a "Published Author's Network" member of the Romance Writers of America and PEN America. She is represented by Kevan Lyon of Marsal Lyon Literary Agency.

www.aleatharomig.com
aleatharomig@gmail.com